ROBOT CITY'S GREATES

CURTIS
THE COLOSSAL
COAST-GUARD ROBOT,
MUST FACE HIS TOUGHEST TEST YET!

MIDNIGHT, ROBOT CITY.
POPULATION: 15 MILLION HUMANS,
1 MILLION ROBOTS.

AS THEY SAY IN
ROBOT CITY, IT'S
RAINING CATS
AND COGS!

OK EVERYONE, THAT'S WHAT I CALL A GOOD DAY'S WORK. LET'S GET THE COFFEE ON AND PUT OUR FEET UP.

BUT IT WASN'T TO BE . . . .

CALLING ROBOT CITY COAST GUARD!

THIS IS THE OIL DRILLING PLATFORM *RED STAR III*. *SOS!*

THIS IS ROBOT CITY COAST GUARD. HOW CAN WE HELP?

WE'VE COME ADRIFT. WE'RE ON FIRE AND WE'RE LEAKING OIL . . . LOTS OF IT!

WAKE UP, BIG GUY. WE'VE GOT A HOT ONE!

UNDERSTOOD, BOB. I'VE INITIATED POWER-UP.

COMMUNICATIONS DECK IS READY FOR THE CREW!

ACTION STATIONS! ACTION STATIONS!

NIGHT CREW, REPORT TO CURTIS. *ON THE DOUBLE!*

HERE WE GO AGAIN!

COME ON, WE'VE GOT TO GET THESE CABLES OFF QUICKLY.

SEAL THAT LEG UNIT UP AS FAST AS YOU CAN!

THE HATCH IS OPEN, BOB. WHAT HAVE WE GOT TONIGHT THEN?

POSSIBLE MAJOR ENVIRONMENTAL DISASTER AND FIRE AT SEA!

# CURTIS THE COLOSSAL COAST-GUARD ROBOT!

30 MILES OFF THE COAST OF ROBOT CITY, THE CREW OF THE RED STAR III OIL RIG ARE GETTING JITTERY. . . .
THE FIRE HAS SPREAD TO C DECK!
IF WE DON'T STOP IT SOON, PUMP SIX WILL BLOW AS WELL.
THIS RIG HAS ONLY BEEN OPERATIONAL FOR FOUR MONTHS. WE SHOULDN'T BE HAVING PROBLEMS YET!
ANY NEWS FROM ROBOT CITY?
I'M NOT PICKING ANYTHING UP, CHIEF. SINCE THE MAIN TRANSMITTER BLEW, IT'S HARD TO GET A CLEAR SIGNAL.
THE RIG ROBOTS ARE MELTING, SIR! THEY'RE TRYING TO PUT OUT THE FIRE.
THEY KEEP ON RUSHING IN WITH NO REGARD FOR THEIR OWN SAFETY.

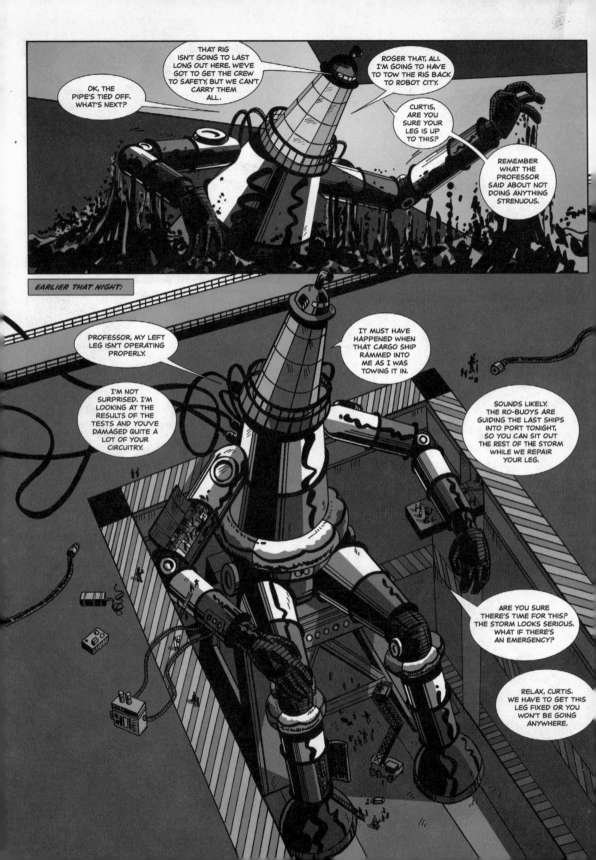

SO WHAT DO YOU THINK, CURTIS? CAN THIS DRAGON CITY ROBOT BEAT SMASH HARRY?

I DON'T KNOW, BOB. I'VE NEVER SEEN SMOKIN' JONES IN ACTION, BUT DRAGON CITY IS PRODUCING SOME REAL TOUGH ROBOTS THESE DAYS.

THAT'S RIGHT, CURTIS. DRAGON TECH INDUSTRIES IS BECOMING A FRONT-RUNNER IN ROBOT DEVELOPMENT.

AFTER ROBOT CITY, OF COURSE.

NATURALLY!

REMEMBER WHEN WE SAW SMASH BEAT THE DEADLY GORILLA?

OH YEAH, WHAT A NIGHT!

WE SURE HAD A BIG OLD PARTY AFTERWARD!

WE'LL PARTY TOMORROW WHEN SMASH WINS AGAIN. SO BRING SOME EXTRA FEET!

DON'T REMIND ME! I STILL CAN'T FIND MY SPARE FEET!

WHO ARE YOU BACKING, JULIE?

OH, SMASH OF COURSE. HE'S ONE HUNKY HUNK OF METAL!

CURTIS, WE'RE UPLOADING NEW SOFTWARE FOR YOUR LEFT LEG.

LEFT LEG READY FOR REBOOT, SIR.

YOU NEED TWENTY-FOUR HOURS IN SLEEP MODE TO FULLY REPAIR YOUR SYSTEMS.

NOW SIT BACK AND RELAX, MY BOY. I DON'T WANT YOU DOING ANYTHING STRENUOUS FOR THE NEXT FEW DAYS.

ROGER THAT, PROFESSOR. NOTHING STRENUOUS . . .

ALL RIGHT, TEAM, I NEED SOME CONCENTRATION NOW. IT LOOKS LIKE WE MIGHT HAVE A TRICKY SITUATION UP AHEAD SO I WANT YOU ALL IN THE ZONE AND ON TOP OF YOUR GAMES.

REMEMBER, THIS IS THE ROBOT CITY COAST GUARD YOU'RE IN!

YES, SIR!

LISTEN TO THOSE RO-BUOYS. IT MAKES ME PROUD TO BE PART OF THE COAST GUARD!

IT SURE DOES, CURTIS.

NUMBER ONE REPORTING IN. WE'RE IN THE ROBERTS RIVER AND WE CAN SEE THE CAUSE OF THE TROUBLE. IT'S BIG AND IT'S GOT TENTACLES!

WE'LL GET CLOSER TO INVESTIGATE.

KEEP ME POSTED. AND BE CAREFUL OUT THERE.

WE DON'T KNOW WHAT WE'RE DEALING WITH. IT MAY BE VERY DANGEROUS.

WHAT ON EARTH CAN THAT THING BE?

AND WHAT DOES IT WANT?

IT'S PROBABLY THAT GROUP OF ROBO-PIRANHAS THAT THE ZOO LOST LAST MONTH.

GROUND CREW, WHATEVER STAGE YOU'RE AT, FINISH UP. WE NEED CURTIS READY TO GO--*NOW!*

LEFT LEG CREW CLOSING UP!

SIR, WE ARE TRACKING THE CREATURE AND IT HAS STOPPED JUST UNDER THE BRIDGE.

I DON'T LIKE THE SOUND OF THAT!

BOB, IT'S THE MORNING RUSH HOUR. THAT BRIDGE WILL BE PACKED WITH PEOPLE!

CHIEF . . .

I'M PICKING UP NEW SIGNALS IN THE WATER--LOOKS LIKE OUR SEA MONSTER'S GOT FRIENDS . . .

COAST GUARD! THIS IS THE RIVER POLICE. WE'VE GOT A . . . A . . . GREAT BIG THING WITH TENTACLES TRYING TO PULL DOWN WEST ISLAND WAY BRIDGE!

I HEARD THAT!

BIG GUY . . .

I'M GOOD TO GO WITH WHAT I'VE GOT!

IT'S WORKING. THEY'RE ALL COMING WITH ME--EVEN THE BIG ONE!

CURTIS, WE HAVE ORDERS TO BOMB THE SEA CREATURES IF YOU THINK THEY ARE A THREAT TO THE CITY.

UNDERSTOOD BLUE FLIGHT, BUT HOLD FIRE FOR NOW. THEY SEEM CONTENT TO JUST FOLLOW.

CURTIS, ALL THE CREATURES HAVE CLEARED THE RIVER. BUT YOU'RE ATTRACTING MARINE LIFE FROM ALL OVER.

WHAT CAN I SAY, BLUE FLIGHT? IT'S MY SHEER MECHANICAL MAGNETISM.

I'VE NEVER BEEN SO POPULAR! I'M PICKING UP SOME SIGNALS NOW-- THEY'RE MAKING A LOT OF NOISE DOWN THERE.

YOU ARE HEADING TOWARD THE *RED STAR III* DRILLING FIELD.

CURTIS, WE ARE ALMOST ON TOP OF THE DRILL HOLE.

TRY CHANGING THE FREQUENCY YOU'RE BROADCASTING ON TO SEE WHAT HAPPENS.

CURTIS, WHAT'S HAPPENING?
WELL--IT'S A LITTLE HARD TO EXPLAIN.
IN FACT, EVEN I DON'T BELIEVE IT. THE ANIMALS ARE SPEAKING TO ME!
HELLO, BIG TIN MAN!
NOW IT'S CALMER I CAN SEE MUCH BETTER DOWN HERE THAN LAST NIGHT . . .
AND IT'S NOT A PRETTY SIGHT. THERE'S LOADS OF TRASH AND THERE'S STILL A MASSIVE OIL LEAK! I THOUGHT I'D TIED IT OFF. . . .

THE NEXT DAY IN ROBOT CITY:

HE'S DONE IT AGAIN!

READ ALL ABOUT IT! CURTIS SAVES ROBOT CITY! MAYOR BACKS WAVE-POWER RESEARCH! READ ALL ABOUT IT!

THAT'S ROBOT CITY INGENUITY FOR YOU. NO ONE BEATS OUR ROBOTS!

WHAT A HERO. HE'S STILL OUT THERE LEADING THE CLEANUP AND NEGOTIATING WITH THE SEA CREATURES.

THAT BIG OLD WALKING, TALKING LIGHTHOUSE NEVER LET US DOWN!

AND SO, AFTER FIVE DAYS OUT AT SEA HELPING CLEAN UP AFTER THE OIL LEAK, CURTIS IS PREPARING TO DIVE ONCE AGAIN FOR MORE PEACE TALKS WITH THE MARINE LIFE.

EARLIER TODAY, HE HAD A FEW WORDS FOR ROBOT CITY NEWS.

... AFTER ALL, AS A COAST-GUARD OFFICER I'M DUTY-BOUND TO ENSURE THE SAFETY NOT ONLY OF OUR CITY'S SHIPS, BUT ALSO THE CREATURES WHO LIVE BENEATH THE WAVES.

WELL SAID.

AND THE BEST OF ROBOT LUCK TO HIM.

THERE HE GOES, WORKING HARD TO ENSURE PEACE BETWEEN ROBOT-, HUMAN-, AND MARINE-KIND.

IT MUST BE A DIFFICULT AND DELICATE JOB TRYING TO NEGOTIATE WITH ANOTHER SPECIES.

HOW DO YOU RECKON HE WILL APPROACH IT?

I WOULD IMAGINE CURTIS WILL FOLLOW STANDARD PROCEDURES, KEEPING TO THE POINT IN AN EFFICIENT AND RESPECTFUL MANNER, WHILE AT ALL TIMES MAINTAINING A DIGNIFIED PROFESSIONAL ATTITUDE.

THE END